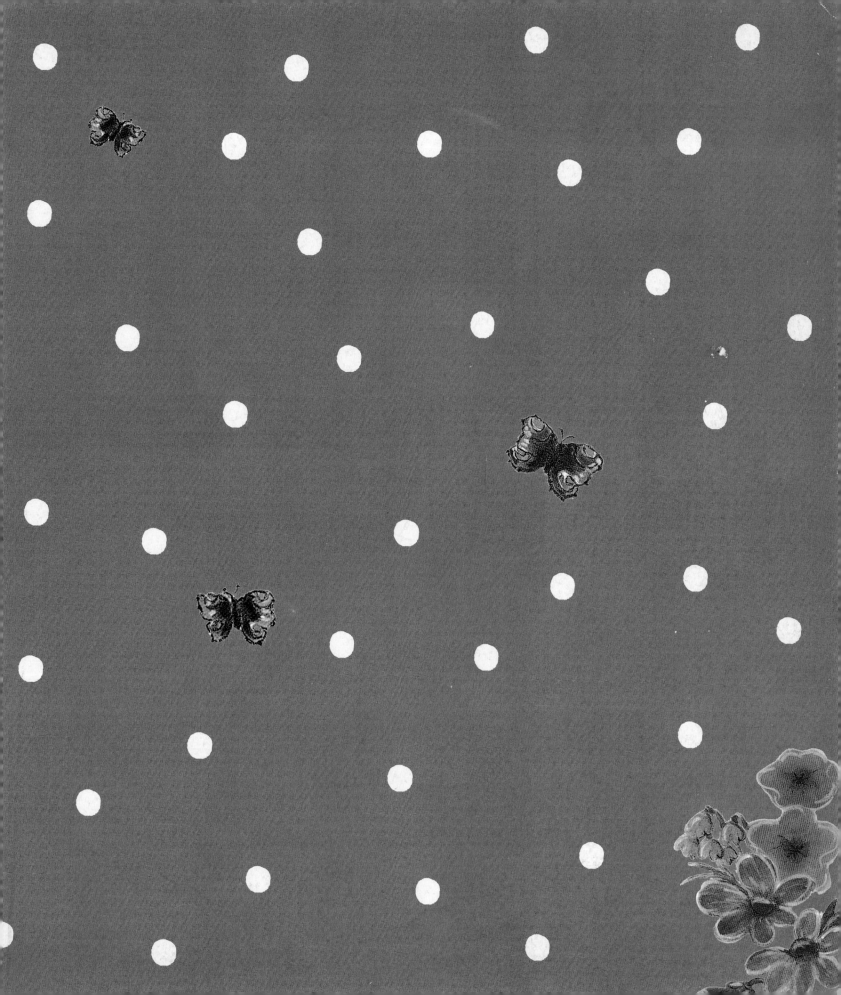

For Thea, with love
P.R. & E.R.

ORCHARD BOOKS
96 Leonard Street, London EC2A 4XD
*Orchard Books Australia*
32/45-51 Huntley Street, Alexandria, NSW 2015
ISBN 1 84121 438 8 (hardback)
ISBN 1 84362 360 9  (paperback)
First published in Great Britain in 2004
First paperback publication in 2005
Text © Paul Rogers 2004
Illustrations © Emma Rogers 2004
The right of Paul Rogers to be identified as the author
and Emma Rogers to be identified as the illustrator of
this work has been asserted by them in accordance
with the Copyright, Designs and Patents Act, 1988.
A CIP catalogue record for this book is available from the British Library.
(hardback) 10 9 8 7 6 5 4 3 2 1
(paperback) 10 9 8 7 6 5 4 3 2 1
Printed in Singapore

# Little Dancer

## Paul and Emma Rogers

ORCHARD BOOKS

I wake up in the morning
And straight away I know,
Today will be a dancing day
Everywhere I go!

I pirouette
in puddles.

I skip along
the street.

I prance all round the garden
With nothing on my feet.

I strut just like a peacock.

I stretch just like a cat.

I flutter like a butterfly
(I'm really good at that!)

I hop just like
a rabbit.

I gallop like
a horse.

I'm all those different animals,
But I'm still me, of course!

I go to ballet classes
On Fridays with my friend.
I'm the greatest dancer there
(Or that's what I pretend).

"Point your toes," they tell you,
"Back straight, lift your chin.
Nice and graceful, shoulders down,
Tuck your tummy in."

Although I'm good at whirling
And hardly ever fall,

Not wobbling when you stop
Is still the hardest thing of all!

And when the lesson's over,
If it's a sunny day,
We go back home together –
Dancing all the way.

A proper ballerina –
That's what I want to be.

Up goes the curtain
And who's there . . . ?

Me!

I tiptoe in my tutu.
The music fills my ears.

And when I do my biggest jump,
Everybody cheers.

I step into the spotlight
And throw the crowd a kiss.
And as the flowers come raining down,
I curtsey – just like this.

Then when I've had my supper
And when it's time for bed,

I slip into my shoes and have
A last quick twirl with Ted.

And now the daylong dancing
Is over, so it seems.

But though I may be fast asleep . . .

. . . I'm dancing
in my dreams!

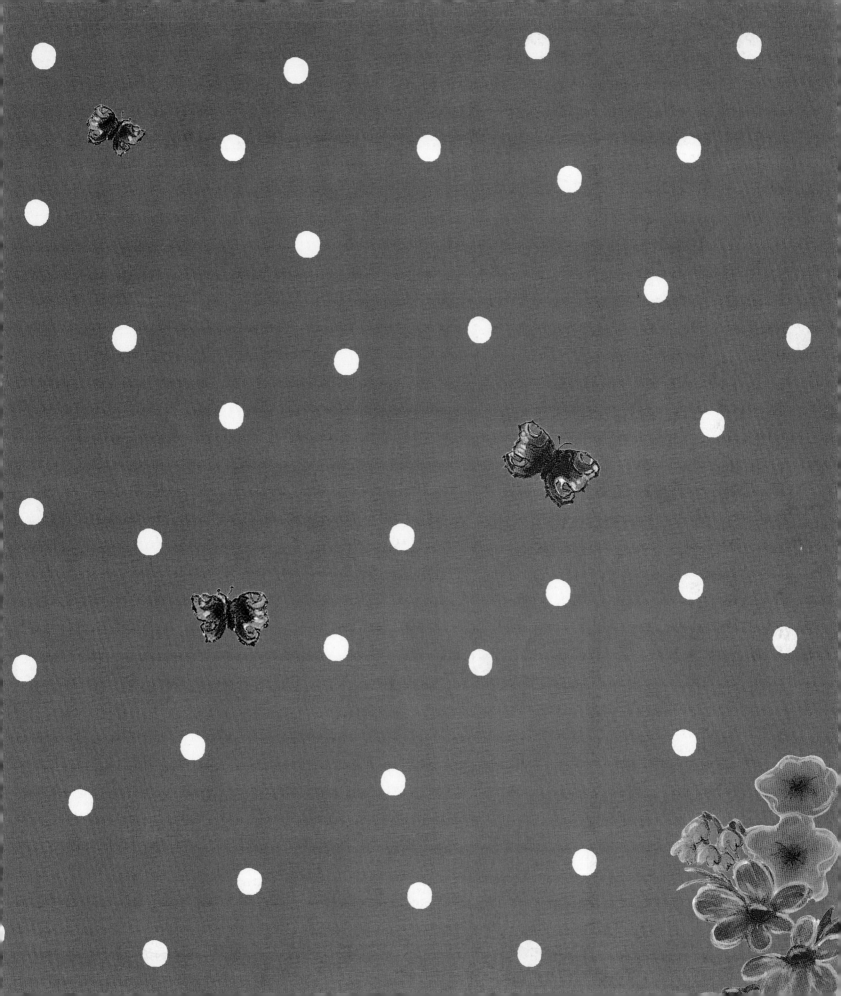